WALKS TALL THE
MOON

To Lynn,

Best Wishes

Dedicated to the Teachers for the love and effort they put into each student.

WALKS TALL THE MOON

LEARNING MINDFULNESS

Robert Bollendorf

Illustrator: Frank Salvatini

urlink
PRINT & MEDIA

1603 Capitol Ave., Suite 310 Cheyenne, Wyoming USA 82001
1-888-980-6523 | admin@urlinkpublishing.com

URLink Print and Media is committed to excellence in the publishing industry.

Published in the United States of America

ISBN 978-1-64367-418-6 (Paperback)
ISBN 978-1-64367-417-9 (Digital)

24.04.19

INTRODUCTION

My dear children and grandchildren this is the first story of Tall Moon— how he got his name and his early struggles and adventures.

It is hard to say exactly when Tall Moon lived, but it was before radio and TV, not to mention cell phones and computers.

From here on, just let the story flow over you.

The exercises come from something called mindfulness. I hope you will read it as a family and that you learn what Tall Moon learns. After you have gone through the story, pick out one or two of the exercises he does and do them every day just for a minute or two. Maybe take a walk in the woods and do some of the things Tall Moon does with *your* family. If you do them, science says you will actually increase the size and ability of parts of your brain that help you to make good decisions— like what to put into your body, whether to walk toward or away from certain people, places and things.

Thousands of people live in pain every day from their choices to use drugs. Even food can be eaten in ways that harm their bodies. Also what they choose to say or do to someone else can cause themselves pain as well as others.

Hopefully if you are willing to take a minute or two out of your day to use what you are about to learn, you can decrease the choices you make that lead to bad consequences.

You will also decrease the activity of parts of your brain that are involved in panic, anxiety, sadness, anger, and fear. Take this journey with me now and travel in the seven directions Indians believe in: north, south, east, west, up, down, and within.

Tall Moon

CHAPTER 1

Tall Moon sat in the long house, his legs folded and his back straight; only his face and hair gave a hint of his age. He had deep lines on his face from years of living through cold winters and hot summers, and he had long white hair.

He had entered the long house through the east door, where the sun rises. And when he would leave, it would be where the sun set, through the west door. There was a small fire in the middle of the long house with a small hole in the roof to let the smoke out. The tribe lined the sides waiting to hear another story from Tall Moon. The long house is where the ceremonies such as the naming ceremony took place, but also where the stories were told that helped the tribe understand their heritage and those of other tribes. Tall Moon told stories about the Menominee and Mohican Indians, and about the tribes that lived in North, Central, and South

America for at least 10,000 years. Tall Moon believed they always had lived here and recent discoveries show there are bones of humans as far back as a million years in the Americas.

Tall Moon taught them the Navaho's belief the first man and first woman came to earth from the lower regions through a reed. Some tribes in what is now Mexico believed they came from the stars. He talked about early beliefs like the earth was really on the back of a large turtle. The Menominee believe the Great Spirit changed a light skinned bear into a human, and then did the same with a wolf, an eagle, a crane, and a moose creating the five clans of the Menominee.

Tall Moon came from the Turtle clan, which is a clan of his grandfather who came to the Menominee from the Mohican tribe. Tall Moon told stories of the olden days when the Menominee once held most of the land in northern Wisconsin from Oshkosh to Canada and from Lake Michigan as far west as the Mississippi. Tall Moon told them that it was always difficult to clearly distinguish exactly where the territory of most Indian tribes was because they didn't believe in land ownership or mapping out clear boundaries. He told them that before the white man arrived there were Indian tribes living in every state of the United States.

One evening one of the younger members of the tribe asked Tall Moon "I'm grateful for all you have taught us about the origins of our people, but tonight could you tell us about your origin? What do you think caused you to become so wise?" Embarrassed by the question, Tall Moon told the story as if he were speaking of someone else.

CHAPTER 2

He was born in early fall, at a time when the days were still warm, but the nights were cool and longer, and the trees were just beginning to show their fall colors. The time when days were getting shorter and a blanket provided welcome warmth at night. The fires were not just for cooking but felt good in the hour of storytelling before bedtime.

It was early evening when his mother felt tightness in her belly telling her the baby was ready to face the world. She and the tribal women went into the teepee while his father and brothers and his sisters waited outside.

When one of his aunts brought him out to show him to his father, the moon was just rising over the water where they lived. It was full and golden and shimmered on the water. When his father raised him up to get a look, the moon was to his father's back. The moon shone in the infant's eyes and he cast a long shadow on the ground behind him. His father noticed this and decided to call him Tall Moon. Tall Moon grew with his family. He was the youngest and was lucky to have been born, since his mother had lived through forty winters by the time she had him.

His mother was more protective of him than with her other children since she knew he would be her last child.

When his brothers would go out hunting with his father, Tall Moon would stay back with his mother and sisters. It was not that he didn't learn the ways of men, he may have been the best shot with a bow and arrow of all the boys his age and older— but that was mostly shooting rabbits and squirrels. He had little experience killing big game.

He had his bow with him in the fall of his 11th year when his mother and he were out hunting for the last berries of the season. Without knowing it, they came between a mother bear and her cubs, something a mother bear would never allow. The mother bear charged, coming toward them on her hind legs.

He raised his bow to shoot, but just then the bear dropped to all fours and the shot that would have hit the bear's heart sailed over her head.

The bear was nearly on top of him before he could pull another arrow from his quiver.

"Go!" Tall Moon's mother screamed as she stepped in between Tall Moon and the bear. To Tall Moon, time seemed too slow and every detail rushed at him. As he raced toward the village, he ran by the cubs and noticed one of the cubs had as blond streak on one of his shoulders.

Tall Moon screamed as he neared the village "Help!" His father and brothers met him before he got there.

Totally out of breath, he pointed. Looking at the terror in Tall Moon's face, his father jumped and ran into the woods.

He followed Tall Moon's footprints and soon reached the bear. With one shot the bear was dead, but it was too late for Tall Moon's mother.

***

After that things changed in Tall Moon's family. Though his father never said it directly, Tall Moon was sure that his father blamed him for his mother's death. Tall Moon's brothers and sister had to pick up the duties of their mother. Their father was often gone too, trying to ease his grief by wandering alone in the woods. There was little time to spend as a family.

As for Tall Moon, he seemed afraid of the woods and stayed close to the village. When he ventured into the woods, the smallest noise would make him anxious.

He did not hunt and when it was time to thank their brother animals for giving their lives so the people of the village could live, Tall Moon was silent.

In his heart, Tall Moon believed it was an animal that took his mother's life. He had no compassion for them, nor did he have any for himself. Luckily for him there were aunties* and uncles* who cared for him.

*Indian's believe all elders were their aunties or uncles even animals were their brothers. Old people were honored as grandmothers or grandfathers. Even the moon was called grandmother and rocks were called grandfathers.

CHAPTER 3

Then there was school. School was a struggle. Tall Moon attended a mission school. It was much better than the schools other Indians attended which were far away from their families and forced them to give up their Indian names, and made them speak English rather than honoring their culture and language.

In school, Tall Moon was always daydreaming. He would imagine he was riding with Sitting Bull at Little Big Horn, or he was with Geronimo, or Chief Oshkosh standing up to the white man to make his father proud.

But the teachers would run out of patience while they tried to teach him math or science or English. His mind would always be somewhere else. One teacher in particular tried everything to get Tall Moon to pay attention, besides repeating over and over "On the Moon" (her nick name for him) pay attention.

She would sneak up behind him when he had that faraway look and fill a bag full of air and then pop it behind him. Then all his class- mates would laugh as he jumped from his seat.

Yet Tall Moon would continue to travel to another place and time.

Sometimes after recess, she would say to the entire class, "Now settle down and pay attention." That never seemed to work.

At the end of school in his 12th year the elders of the tribe including his father, spoke of Tall Moon around the fire. They all agreed that education was a ladder Tall Moon had to climb, and they saw in him great potential. They also agreed that they needed to do something to help his pain. They decided even though he was still quite young, that he might benefit from a Vision Quest.

His Aunt Robin Egg (named for her piercing blue eyes), and Uncle Deep Waters would prepare him for the quest. Then the elders would observe him from out of sight in case he was in danger.

CHAPTER 4

Aunt Robin Egg and Uncle Deep Waters set the Vision Quest for right after school dismissed for summer.

They told Tall Moon there were three important elements to a Vision Quest: fasting, solitude and nature. He learned that he would be taken deep in the forest without food or water. He was not to eat or drink for the first day and night. After that, he could only have small amounts of liquid and plants he found in the woods. On the morning of the fourth day, he was to make his own way back to the village where all would be waiting to hear of his adventures.

It was his Uncle Deep Waters who escorted him to the spot where he would camp. They started out from the village early in the morning after Tall Moon had some food. They walked all day, mostly in silence.

His uncle would occasionally point out spots to remember in finding his way back. On the way, he asked his uncle what he should do to make his quest successful, even though he held out little hope that he would gain anything but insect bites.

His uncle advised, "Well, you must pay attention.

Here we go again Tall Moon thought as his mind flashed back to school. "Pay attention! Pay attention! Pay attention!" he heard every teacher he'd ever had echoing in his head. What was supposed to happen next was what confused Tall Moon.

But then his Uncle continued, "Pay attention to what is happening right now. Pay attention to what is happening inside your body. Notice how you are breathing or how parts of your body feel. Do that with acceptance and without judgment. If your mind wanders just bring your focus back to what is happening now and never criticize yourself if your mind does wander." Tall Moon still wasn't sure what any of that meant, but at least it was more than he knew before.

CHAPTER 5

His Uncle left him in a clearing on the ridge of a high hill. His uncle had previously visited the spot and added plenty of firewood and cleared a soft spot for sleeping. He also left what Tall Moon would need for making meals. There was a stream that wound its way around the hill just down an incline from where he set up his deerskins.

One skin underneath to keep the cold ground from his body and one to protect him from the night air. It was a warm night, so cold was not his concern. He crawled under his deerskin and looked at the sky. Once away from the village and the campfires, there were more stars than he had ever seen; and with just a sliver of a moon there was nothing to hide their brilliance.

Tall Moon focused mostly on his hunger. He had not eaten since morning and he wondered how he would ever get to sleep with the constant thought of food. All the sounds the night made him aware he was alone. Being alone always made him remember the day his mother died. He wished he had never gone with his mother that day. He wished he would have killed the bear or the bear had killed him. He wished the elders would just leave him alone and not try and help. All this thinking made him miserable.

He tried to remember his uncle's words. "Pay attention to what is happening inside you."

How would that help? All it did was to make him focus even more on how hungry he was and at how mad he was at the elders for putting him through this.

Then he remembered three other things...

Focus on now, bring your mind back and don't judge. He focused his attention on his belly and when he did that he noticed it rose up and down with his breath.

Then he concentrated on his breath. He noticed that if he breathed slowly and deeply, he felt calmer. After a couple of breaths, he concentrated on his stomach again. He noticed he still had the pain of hunger but it had changed. It was still there, but not as painful.

That is when Tall Moon made two more discoveries:

First, he realized pain changes.

Second, there was a difference between pain and suffering. The pain in his stomach was turned into suffering by adding to it in his own mind. He focused on his breathing again and he noticed his breath was quieter and slower. He also noticed that focusing on his breathing slowed his mind down. His calm body and the exhaustion from the long walk through the woods caught up to him and soon he fell asleep.

CHAPTER 6

Tall moon awoke to the sun just rising over the trees and the sound of birds singing.Then he remembered where he was, and what his purpose was.

At that very moment he yawned and stretched and noticed his breathing had changed. He decided to stretch again and see how it felt. He tried to remember his dreams, but he slept so soundly that he couldn't remember any.

He still marveled at how just paying attention to his breathing made a difference to his pain.

Breathing was something he did day and night since he was born; yet when he paid attention to it, there was something different. He tried focusing on his breathing again, but this time his mind wandered to how he would spend the next three days.

When he recognized that he had left the moment, he brought his mind back.

He started to feel bad, but he remembered his uncle's words – "Never criticize yourself if your mind wanders."

He thought to himself "How can I keep my mind in the moment?" He was stretching when he started breathing, so he decided to try stretching again.

This time he did a stretch like a half of a snow angel.

As he raised his arms up, he took a deep breath in and as he lowered them back to his side, he let his breath out. This seemed to help him keep his focus on the present.

Next he laced his fingers behind his head. As he breathed in, he lowered his elbows down to the ground and as he breathed out, he raised them toward his ears. Finally, he decided to survey his body. The first thing he noticed was that his hunger was gone. The next thing he noticed was that he was very thirsty. So he pulled back his covers, went to the stream, and took a drink. The morning had a chill in the air so he filled a bucket the elders provided, took it back to his camp, and heated some water on the fire he had built. He walked around in the woods and found some herbs that his mother had taught him to use and he added them to the hot water. When the water was hot, he poured it in his cup and sat by the fire. He held the cup in both hands and smelled the aroma of the herbs. He took a sip, but it was still hot, so he blew gently on the liquid. That is when he realized he had learned still another way to focus on his breathing. Breathing in, he smelled the herbs through his nose. Breathing out, he held his mouth like a kiss and blew softly on his brew.

After he finished his drink, he decided since this would be his home for three days he should decorate it.

He drew a medicine wheel in the dirt with his finger. The wheel was about as big as his hand. It had four equal parts like a pie cut into quarters. He couldn't color the pieces black, yellow, red, and white to represent the four races, but the drawing gave him another idea for breathing. He put his finger on the top of the circle and breathed in, when his finger reached the end of the first quarter, he breathed out, when his finger reached the bottom of the circle he breathed in, half way up the other side he breathed out until he was back at the top of the circle.

He watched his hand as he followed the circle and decided to trace his hand in the dirt. He placed his left hand down in the dirt and with his right hand began to trace his left hand. He started at the bottom of his thumb. As his right finger moved up the outside of his thumb he breathed in. When it reached the top, he paused and breathed out as his right finger moved down his thumb toward his index finger. He did this until his finger moved down the outside of his little finger.

He picked up his hand from the dirt and decided to trace it back the other way with his left hand in the air. He did this several times and was excited to find still other ways he could keep focused on the present.

Tall Moon decided to take a walk and as soon as he did, he began to ask himself:

"What if I get lost?"

"How will I find my way back?"

"I wonder if I am not supposed to leave camp?"

Then Tall Moon stopped, took a breath, and observed where he was. "If I follow the stream, I can't get lost. This is my quest, I'm going to do it my way!" he said to himself.

He had already learned so much, how could this be wrong? Tall Moon realized he had just learned something new that he could use forever. STOP, TAKE A BREATH, OBSERVE, PROCEED.

CHAPTER 7

As Tall Moon walked on, he was determined to try to stay in the present moment and expand his awareness to the outside environment as well. He started with what he could see. He sat on a rock and closed his eyes, so he could start as if seeing the world around him for the first time. When he opened his eyes, he saw a forest that was alive with the colors of late spring and early summer. Tall Moon was amazed with how many different greens he saw. He noticed some of the trees were just beginning to leaf out and the leaves were still light green as opposed to those trees that had reached their summer's best that were dark green. He noticed the pine trees varied in green. Some were almost light blue, others different shades of green. He noticed the

blue sky, and the clear steam with different colored rocks underneath. He observed the white and pink blossoms on wild flowers.

When he saw birds flying from tree to tree, he decided to switch to what he could hear. The first sound he heard was the song of the red bird. The melody changed several times, as he tried to impress a mate with his musical ability. He heard the sharp jay of the blue bird.

Each call was unique.

He tried not to judge one as beautiful and one not, but simply to appreciate the variety of sound. He heard the chirp of the red-breasted bird, the wail of a loon on a nearby lake and the peep of the tiny frogs in the swamp nearby.

As he concentrated on the swamp, he couldn't help but notice the potent smell of the swamp, so he decided to focus on what he could smell. He sniffed deeply. The clean smell of the woods counteracted the decaying smell of the swamp. The pine trees smelled clean and fresh, but he also caught a faint smell of a skunk protecting himself with his scent. Tall moon was glad the skunk wasn't closer and had a hard time not judging the scent.

It was then Tall Moon noticed his old friend hunger rearing its head so he started to concentrate on how he felt. First he felt an ant crawling on his arm, then a gentle breeze, followed by the warm sun on his face. He had been sitting on a rock while he concentrated on his senses and noticed the rock was beginning to feel hard. The muscles in his arms tensed as he pushed against the rock and the muscles in his legs contracted as he stood to begin searching for food. He found some fresh asparagus growing in the woods. He decided to pick it to take it back to camp and cook. He ate a raw piece on his way back and concentrated on how the taste changed as he continued to chew. Along the way, he found some wild strawberries. The contrast in taste was remarkable.

He started another fire, boiled some water, and cooked the asparagus. When he ate the cooked asparagus, he remembered how crunchy the raw asparagus tasted. The texture of the cooked asparagus was soft and stringy. "How can a little hot water make them so different?" Tall Moon thought.

CHAPTER 8

After he ate, Tall Moon heard a loon's call, and realized a lake must be nearby. He knew streams flow into lakes, so he followed the stream until he found the lake.

Tall Moon sat by the water. At first, when he arrived, there was no wind. The lake was a mirror for all that surrounded it. The cool green pine trees, the white fluffy clouds, even the birds high in the sky were so accurately reflected in the water that Tall Moon could look down and see the same thing as when he looked up. Close by were some fruit trees with blossoms still clinging to the branches. Every once in a while, a blossom would float down towards the water. Tall Moon watched it rocking back and forth, back and forth until it hit the water with a tiny tap. He watched the circles flow out from it, as even that little disturbance caused a

ripple in the lake. He then saw his own refection in the lake. At that moment, he and the lake became one.

He picked up a rock.

"Hello Grandfather Rock" he said. "Would you mind going for a swim?"

He took the rock's silence as approval and threw it toward the middle of the lake. He watched the ripples flow out in perfect circles in all directions. He imagined that those circles were flowing everywhere inside of him. Starting at his tummy, the ripples soothed and quieted every muscle and every organ in his body. When the ripples reached his brain, it too was quieted.

Then he imagined the rock sinking to the bottom. He imagined storms on the surface of the water and yet where the rock sat it was calm.

He imagined the changing seasons even winter when the lake froze the rock did not change; perhaps he too could have a spot inside himself that did not change no matter what happened around him.

Tall Moon sat for a long time with his eyes closed, feeling the rock in his hand and in his mind. When he opened his eyes, the lake was no longer calm. At the far end of the lake, a wind was blowing hard enough so that the lake was now wavy. The waves came and went from the shore. Tall Moon returned to his breathing and matched it to the waves rolling in and out, in and out.

Was there something, he thought, that connected all things?

For the first time in a while he thought of his mother. Was she now a part of the one of all things? Tall Moon had no answer, but for the first time when he thought of his mother, he felt peace. Again he remained for a long time with his thoughts. When he looked around he noticed the sun looked as if it were about to take a swim as it was nearly setting at the other end of the lake. He rose slowly and walked back to camp, occasionally stopping to pick some food to eat. By the time he arrived back at his camp, it was dark. Tall Moon lit a small fire, cooked and ate his food. Then he laid down in his bedroll. He expected to lay there for a long time before falling asleep, but sleep soon overtook him and he sorted the day out in his dreams.

CHAPTER 9

Tall Moon woke with the warm bright sun shining on him. The thoughts of yesterday soon filled his head and he wondered what today would bring. He rose and went quickly to the stream for a cool drink. He again sat and concentrated on his breath. He hadn't made his herb drink yet, but just imagined he held it in his hand, breathing in the aroma and blowing out softly to cool it down. Then he tried some medicine wheel breaths. Finally he did his stop, take a breath, observe, and proceed.

When he looked around he noticed the trees and thought how they breathed. He had learned in science that the trees breathe through their leaves. So Tall Moon stood and raised his arms. As he breathed in, he imagined that he was getting his air through the tips of his fingers. He could even feel them tingle as he did that. He felt the air travel down to his lungs and into his belly. Then he imagined he could push his breath into his feet and grow his own roots right into the ground. He decided this was his favorite breath of all and soon his whole body felt alive.

CHAPTER 10

After gathering a little food and eating it by the fire, Tall Moon decided to walk in the direction taking him even further away from his village. He decided to concentrate on his walk, how did his feet make contact with the ground?

He noticed how his heel struck first, and how his foot rolled forward towards the ball of his foot and finally his toes bent forward.

He noticed how his arms swung slowly at his side, opposite of his legs. He held his bow lightly in one hand and it too swung like the other hand, but opposite.

He walked like that way for a while, paying attention to his surroundings. Like the day before, he started with what he could see, and then switched to his hearing.

He heard the birds singing first, and then a sound that sent a feeling of terror through his body.

Though it was still new to him, he worked hard to apply his new learning. He stopped, and silently took a breath, then observed. What he saw was the cub with the blond stripe on his shoulder.

Several things he observed helped him relax just a little. The cub, like Tall Moon had grown. But the cub had grown much more. He was on the other side of the stream a good distance away. He was up wind from where Tall Moon was standing, which meant he probably didn't smell Tall Moon. The bear seemed involved in reaching a beehive high in a tree.

Tall Moon thought to himself "This time I will not miss!"

Silently, he drew an arrow from his quiver. He strung the arrow to his bow and took aim. As he was about to release the arrow, he stopped.

Of all the animals of the forest, this was perhaps the closest to Tall Moon's brother. They had both lost their mother on the same day and lived the same pain of being alone.

Tall Moon lowered his bow. More aware than ever of his walk, he silently moved on. He was not going to use the bear for food, but maybe he could take something else from the bear. He raised his hands high in the air and growled like a bear. In the north woods of Wisconsin there was nothing as strong as a bear, and Tall Moon began to feel that strength inside him.

If walking like a bear, gave him strength maybe he could learn other lessons from his brother and sister animals. He began to move with the grace of a deer, jumping over fallen logs. Then he stalked like a wolf feeling the safety of the pack running with him. He imagined he was the Alfa Wolf, the leader of the pack . He felt the dominance, but also the responsibility for the care of the pack. Next he tried to move like a moose. With his long legs, he didn't have to jump logs, he could just step over them. He tried to feel what it would be like to have a large rack of horns on his head.

From the moose he took power. He climbed a high hill and found a tree there and then climbed all the way to the top. He spread his arms like they were wings and felt the soaring feeling of an eagle. From the eagle he took vision and freedom. He climbed down the tree and then he waded in the steam raising one of his legs high, looking for fish like a crane. He stood on one leg and tried to balance. A couple of times he almost fell but each time he got better and soon he was standing for a long time on one leg. From the crane he took balance. He now felt the power of the five tribes of the Menominee.

Tall Moon looked up and the sun was already beginning to set. He turned around and walked back to his camp, picking up some food along the way. When he got back to camp he started a fire, boiled some water, and added asparagus, young cattail roots, and herbs. He ate slowly, tasting each bite as he chewed and concentrated on the taste. He cleaned up camp, crawled in his covers, and went to sleep.

CHAPTER 11

When he woke the next morning it was cloudy with just a few patches of blue, but there was no sign of immediate rain. Tall Moon lay there for a while and looked at the images the clouds made or at least what his imagination made of them. He traced his five fingers. He breathed in on his way up a finger and breathed out as he moved down. He placed his hand so it was silhouetted by the glow of the dawn. Tall Moon hoped when he got back to the village and school in the fall, he could keep at least some of the peace he felt now. He vowed to continue to use the breaths he had learned every day.

This time when he went to the stream, he rinsed his face with cold water from the stream. He decided he would eat and drink on his way back to the village. He rolled up his pack, put his few camping supplies inside, tied it and slung it around his shoulder along with his arrows.

On his way back, he again practiced what he could observe through his senses. He tried walking like some more animals. He started with the turtle, which was his grandfather's clan. He walked very slowly and deliberately. Soon he felt anxious to move faster, but he kept at it and learned a little about being patient and enjoying the journey.

Then he decided to walk with different human emotions and characteristics. He started with anxiety and walked fast and back and forth with no purpose. It reminded him of the squirrel that darts back and forth when someone is coming.

Then he walked with anger making an angry look on his face, stomping his feet hard onto the ground, and punching the air with his fists as he moved his arms forward.

Next he did a sad walk lowering his head and shoulders, barely swinging his arms, and taking small steps.

Tall Moon noticed that with each way that he walked, he soon began to feel that way inside. He began to think about what he wanted to show when he walked into his village.

He started out by trying to walk proud. He puffed out his chest and raised his head looking up at the tree tops and down his nose at Mother Earth. He took bold steps, pointing his toes slightly out. He thought he was proud of what he had accomplished, but didn't think this fit with what he wanted to show the people he cared about.

Next he lowered his eyes a little like he was talking to someone. He shortened his stride just a little and pointed his toes straight ahead. He swung his arms easily at his side. The feeling that followed was confidence and it made Tall Moon feel tall. He liked that way of walking and walked that way for a while.

He just had one more thing to do before he reached the village. "Deep Water and Father, please come out now," he called. "I'd like to enter the village with you."

Deep Water and his father came out from behind a tree shaking their heads and feeling embarrassed. "Did you know we were with you all along?"

"I had a suspicion" Tall Moon said, "and that helped me feel safe trying new things."

"Did you have a vision?" Deep Waters asked.

"I'm not sure." Tall Moon said. "But, I learned to settle down and pay attention. I learned to forgive others and myself. I learned compassion for myself and all living things. I learned to draw strength from the bear, power from the moose, vision and freedom from the eagle, balance from the crane, leadership and responsibility from the wolf. I learned patience from the turtle. I learned to keep a place inside of me always calm and the oneness of all things. I also learned to walk tall."

They both hugged Tall Moon.

For the first time Tall Moon could remember, he looked his father in the eyes. "Father I'm sorry for the part I played in you losing the love of your life."

"If your mother were in that same situation right now she would make the same choice, and I would want her to make that choice. She would be so proud of you right now and so am I. Your name will always be Tall Moon, but from now, to me, you will be Walks Tall the Moon." Tall Moon tried always to honor that name. ©

INTO ACTION

Every day you take about 15,000 breaths are you willing to make some of them mindful breaths or some other mindful activity. This can help you in school, sports, arts and life in general.

I will try one of the following breaths daily:

1. Just concentrating on a breath in and out in the present moment, without judgment
2. A snow angel breath
3. Hands behind head breath
4. A hot beverage breath
5. A tree breath
6. A Medicine Wheel breath
7. A five finger breath

8. Concentrating on the five senses
9. An animal walk
10. A feeling walk
11. Mindful eating
12. Mindful driving
13. Doing a STOP

A hypnotist says when I snap my fingers you will.....

The snapping of the fingers is called an anchor, but you can create your own anchors by simply saying when I do this I will remember to do.... for instance when I first stretch in the morning I will remember to do a snow angel breath.

Here are some other anchors you might agree to try.

1. When I first put my feet on the floor...
2. When I open the blinds...
3. When I'm taking a shower or washing my hair...
4. When I check my cell phone.....
5. When I walk into school or work.....
6. Before a test
7. When arguing with my brother, sister, wife, husband, mother, father
8. During commercials

9. Between games
10. While working out(sit ups, weights, stretches)
11. While driving or riding in the car
12. What other times can you think of...

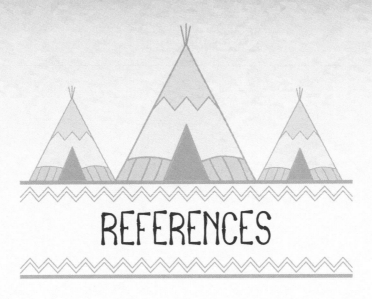

REFERENCES

Though I take full credit for the story of Walks Tall the Moon the mindfulness techniques I have learned from numerous books, workshops and seminars on mindfulness. Here are some of my favorites that you may want to use in your continued journey on the subject:

Alphabreaths: Mindful Breathing for kids Now! By Christopher Willard Ph.D.
Mindful Kids: Activities for Kindness Focus, and Calm By Whitney Stuart and Mina Braun
The Mindfulness Tool Box: 50 Practical Tips, Tools and Handouts for Anxiety, Depression, Stress
   & Pain By Donald Altman, MA, LPC

ACKNOWLEDGEMENTS

First I would like to thank my friends at the College Of Menominee Nation for opportunities to learn about their history and culture especially Debbie Downs and the library staff. I would also like to thank the late Nick Hockings for the opportunities to visit the village he established and to do a sweat lodge.

A few years ago, I took a test to determine my DNA. I was hoping there would be some Native American in me that might explain why I am so attracted to that culture but, alas, I can only call you brothers and sisters in the way you use the term. I guess the other reason is the same reason I used the idea of a vision quest to introduce mindfulness. Ever since I started research for my doctorate degree, I have believed in the value of solitude. I have always loved nature and the North Woods, and been a fan of fasting ever since reading Sidharta by Herman Hesse. So I hope in no way did I disrespect the sacredness of a vision quest by using it as I did, but I could not think of a more ideal way to introduce the subject of mindfulness.

I would also like to thank my dear wife Linda for her numerous readings of this book, and for putting up with my many promises that this is my last book. I would also like to thank Sarah Brown form Eco Gym for sharing my excitement about mindfulness and her enthusiastic endorsement of this story.

I would also like to thank Kathy Quinn Reyes, Barbara Richardson, and David Rutcosky for their support. Finally I would like to thank my children Becky and Bryan for the long journey we have taken together with Walks Tall the Moon that started when they were little and now includes their children. Becky, who is now a reading specialist in the Oswego school system also read the story and made some excellent improvements, not only over all but making it more readable for children.

Finally to my Illustrator and collaborator Frank Salvatini, thanks for your endless patience with me and my lack of computer skills. I value your skills almost as much as your friendship.

CPSIA information can be obtained at www.ICGtesting.com
Printed in the USA
LVIW012042050619
619817LV00001B/1